Windy The Fairy Learns Magic

By Kat Heart

Dedication

This book is dedicated to all the believers, all the dreamers, all the lovers of life who know that magic is everywhere. To those who have ever seen an otherworldly or other dimensional being. To those who have ever felt like they didn't belong yet still allow an open heart and good vibrations to rule their life. People of all ages and all walks of life that realize a positive, collective consciousness is the only way this planet will move forward in sustainability, kindness, and love. This series is for YOU, with gratitude and belief that together we have the ability to create a planet that vibrates pure love.

Thank you for ALWAYS believing in me and helping me to find my sunshine.

Windy is a young Fairy in the village of Oakdale, a mythical and fun Village inside of a majestic and very old oak tree.

In order for fairies to learn how to do many kinds of magic with their wands, they must travel to other fairy villages.

Windy truly wanted to learn all kinds of magic however she was scared to leave her village and her friends.

In order to learn new magic Windy had to move to another fairy village for a while however she didn't feel very brave and was afraid of not knowing anyone in the new village.

Windy's Fairy friends all told her that she would have a wonderful time and love the new village, plus they knew how badly she wanted to learn new magic.

Windy loved her tiny home and beautiful forest decorations, her favorite mushroom table and cute heart shape windows with flowing curtains.

One day she made up her mind to no longer be afraid and go to learn new magic. She packed a bag with some of her favorite things, said goodbye to her friends and set out for the River Creek Fairy Village.

Windy enjoyed her journey even though it took several days. To pass the time as she glided along she picked gum drops and clover, mushrooms and berries, apples and pixie pears.

Best of all were the delicious honey cakes that she traded for at the traveling farmers markets.

RIVER CREEK VILLAGE

When Windy finally reached the River Creek Village she felt happy and was looking forward to her new adventure and the magic she would learn.

It was midday when she arrived and most fairies were out doing fairy things. Windy found the fairy in charge of the School of Fairy Magic and she was given a key to her new home.

As she began to unpack, wondered if she had made a mistake. She was feeling a little down and alone. She thought of her friends and hoped she would make nice, new friends in this village.

When Windy started her new school she felt she wasn't the same as the river fairies. She wanted to make friends but thought maybe she was just too different.

After over a month went by, Windy was learning a lot of new magic but she wasn't really making any new friends.

One thing she loved to do was swim and paddle on leaves. So each day after class Windy went by herself to the beautiful forest creek to play and sing.

One day she noticed a new kind of graceful flying creatures sitting on the edge of the water and watching her with interest.

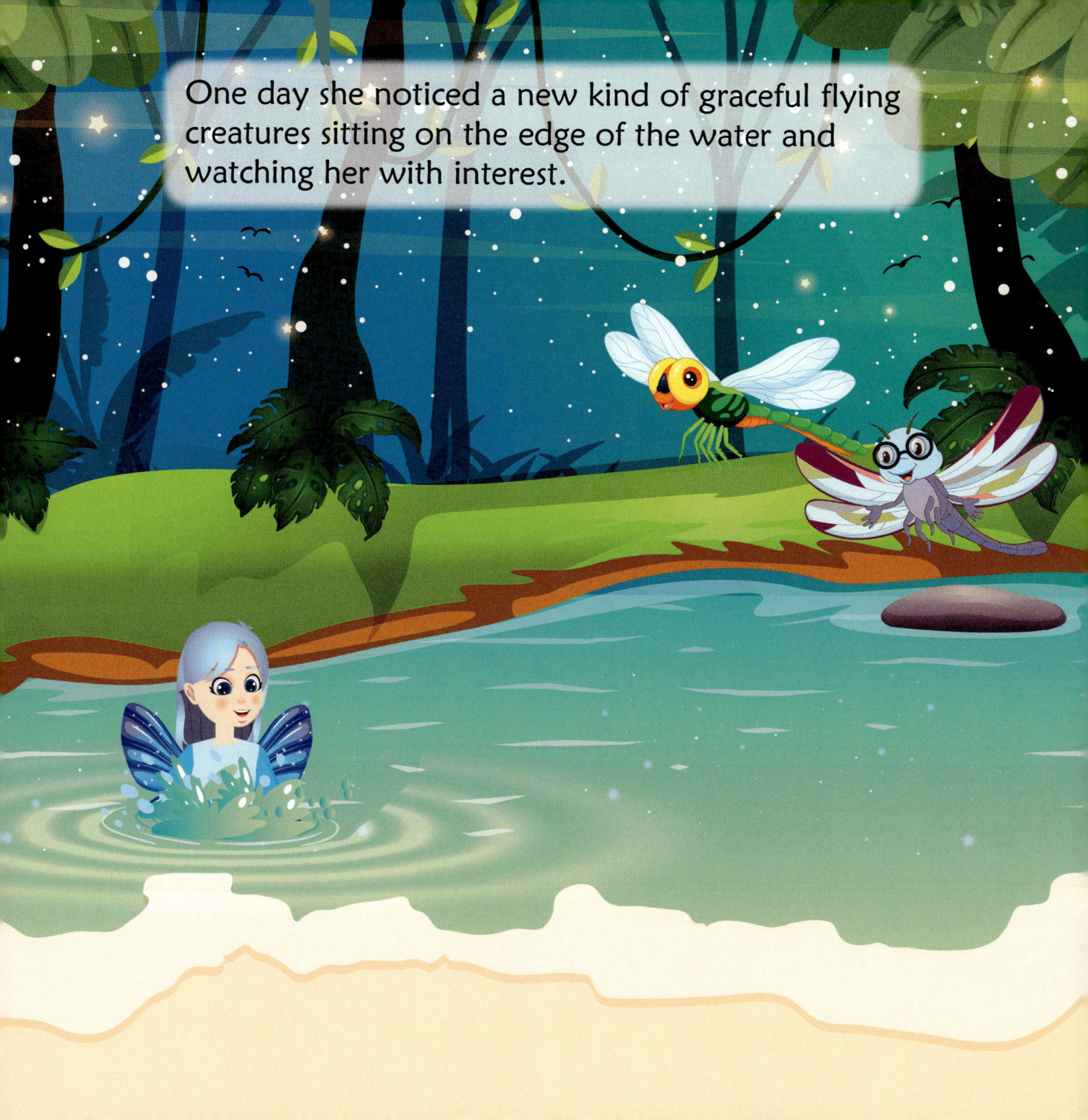

These colorful mini dragon-like creatures were the dragonflies, the source of power and certain kinds of magic for all of River Creek Village. They were the most cherished magical creatures in all the village.

The dragonflies watched Windy while she swam and played and we are delighted by her singing and joyful energy.

One day they came out to play and glide alongside her. As Windy happily watched, the dragonflies flew beside her and hummed while she sang and enjoyed the day…

One of the River Creek fairies, Jupiter, was flying home when he noticed sparkles flying around and heard joyful sounds coming from the creek. He peered over some tall grass and was amazed to see Windy and dragonflies playing together.

Jupiter quickly flew back to the village to tell everyone what he had seen. All the fairies agreed that this had never happened before. They realized that the reason Windy was so different was because she was very magical and special indeed.

When Windy came back home that day, all the river fairies wanted to know about the dragonflies. They sat and listened to her talk for hours and afterward they all went home.

That night Windy sat outside of her new home looked up at the beautiful sky in gratitude. She smiled and thanked the stars above for a very special day.

The End

About the Author

Kat Heart is a dreamer, believer, mystic, and spiritual woman who has a deep passion for people being kind to one another. She is a Fairy Godmother, one on the planet, that works towards helping others to believe in themselves, find forgiveness, and forge the most beautiful future imaginable. She is a traveler, a nature enthusiast, a wanderer, a lover of life, and a passionate soul who will walk through this life with gratitude, childlike wonder and joy! She will always believe in magic, dive into the unknown, support others in their personal beliefs and encourage us all to find that deep and pure love for ourselves so we can share it with our beautiful world.